BACK

(OR WRITE)

Leilac Leamas

*To those who are still foolish enough
to write love letters.*

*This book is for you,
who still believe a letter can change
the course of things.*

*For you who risk the shame of bare paper just to say "come
back," even when you know there won't be an answer.*

*For you, who are naïve enough to write
with your heart, and brave enough to sign with your real name,
or with a name that only she will know how to decipher.*

*This book is for fools—
the last romantics—
who still write love letters.*

That's why they're the only lucid ones.

Prologue

First of all, there is a symbolic amputation: this is not a love story.

Not even letters.

Not even redemption.

This is a hemorrhage contained in paper, so maybe it bleeds slowly, like a razor forgotten in the inside pocket of a jacket. The kind you come back to when you've lost the fight.

People have told me more than once that writing love letters is a sign of weakness.

I disagree.

Weakness is pretending you don't feel it.

Weakness is memorizing speeches about detachment while dreaming of a touch that no longer exists.

Weakness is having words and not using them.

Loving is something else, it's a kind of permitted violence, a vice that cannot be rehabilitated.

I don't know if I've ever been in love. Of course I have—what a stupid thing to say. Of course I've been in love, otherwise I wouldn't be writing this book.

In fact, I don't even know if what I felt was love, or if it was just a well-dressed need, with Italian shoes and ironic promises that life made to me.

I just know that I wrote it.

And that was enough.

Writing has always been my way of pretending to be alive. And if there are letters in this book, it's because there were silences too dense to bear.

The letters are more real than the bodies.

They don't age.

They don't change their scent.

They don't lie afterwards. Yes, after sex.

They only say what they had to say when it was too late.

Like an epitaph that is meant to be loving, but comes out vengeful.

I love poorly.

I write well. I think so, I write well, but there are those who disagree and I don't disagree with those who disagree with me.

And maybe that's how it's always been my punishment.

There is a gap between what you feel and what you can say. This book lives in that gap.

Maybe that's why I seem incoherent, or even pathetic, or too naked.

But if there is something ridiculous here, it's the noble kind. It's the ridicule of someone who isn't ashamed of having loved and failed.

The ridiculousness of those who dared to write, without wanting to save themselves with it.

I'm not a poet. I hate poets.

I'm a man on the run—from others, from myself and from a woman who didn't want to be a character.

I failed in every direction.

But I wrote it down.

So, reader or accomplice, this is for you.

For you, who still write love letters with no addressee.

For you, who folded papers in silence as if they were sentences.

For you, who still believe that there is lucidity in the despair of loving.

It's not a love book.

It's a collection of absences and presences, mistakes and successes, desires and needs.

And maybe—just maybe—an idiotic attempt to come back.

1

Secret Letter
No Location, Undated, Unsigned

Y ou know? I don't know if I'll write to you again. In fact,
     I don't even know if this letter will reach you. Maybe it
     will stay hidden in the false bottom of my Boggi Milano,
which I always carry with me, or maybe I'll drop it in a café in Paris,
between a Negroni and the waiter's distracted gaze.

I'm writing to you because today I dreamt about you... and about
a trial. I don't know if you were there as a lawyer or as a defendant.
Maybe you were both: a defendant lawyer. In the dream, you spoke
with the calm of those who have lost their fear, a bit like me, but
even calmer. I listened to you, like someone reading a forbidden
book by the light of a candle whose wax is slowly melting until it
goes out.

Some days I convince myself that I was made to disappear. Then
there are others when I think that all of this, the lawsuits, the pseu-
donyms, the spy books and their encrypted messages, the others, the
children's books, and the mistresses with city names, is just an idiotic plan to avoid going mad.

I have a real name, as you know. I have accounts in Singapore,
Germany, Italy, Spain, Lithuania and Belize, as you might suspect.
Safe houses where you've already taken refuge with me, and others

where I've taken refuge from you. But what you don't know is that there's a whole dictionary that I only wrote for us. Every time I use the word "labyrinth", I'm saying: "come back". Every time I say "strategy", I'm asking you to "hold me".

But in the end, I'm not asking you for anything. Neither an answer nor love. Just that if you ever find yourself at an airport staring at a boarding gate with no destination and you feel something calling you, well, maybe it's me. But maybe it's just the echo of everything we haven't said to each other and to the world.

Unsigned (by whoever I am today).

2

Reply to Your Letter
Rome, Undated, Signed C.

Leilac -
or Octávio -
or that name you only used when you were naked and surrendered to what you were before you were everyone else,

I read your letter without having received it.

You know there are things that don't need to be delivered to be read. This was one of them. I read it because I knew you were going to write it and I could guess every word.

Yes, I heard your "come back" masquerading as a "labyrinth". I understood the ending you dream of in your "game of hearts".

I read it like someone who recognizes an old note in a new song. And you know what? For a moment, I almost gave in. I almost dropped everything: the meetings; the trial in Rome; Jasmin; and the man who waits for me without really knowing me, as if I were just a prostitute.

But then I remembered you. Of us. What we were when we were together and what we would never fully be, because we never were.

Do you know what you are, Leilac?

An encrypted emotional code that is difficult to solve. A poem written in ink that only appears when it's too late.

You're a hiding place and a trap. And I... I try to escape both.

But don't think I didn't love you.

I loved you with the strength of someone who knows they can't stay. That, and that alone, is why you still exist. Because I keep you in the only place where I can't lose you: my memory.

Keep writing your labyrinths.

Keep teaching Micas to resist.

Keep disappearing in the places where you find yourself again.

But don't wait for me at some airport.

I'm not going back.

Because those who leave without lying don't need to come back to be real.

C., Rome.

3

Unexpected Letter
Vila Nova de Gaia, No date, Signed Leilac

Camilla,
You read a letter that wasn't meant for you. But it was. Because you, as always, are part of what I write, even when I don't write to you.

The letter, the one you found the draft of in my secret place, among erased receipts and mission codes in countries where we no longer live, was for a different woman who no longer exists in my life. Or rather, to one who existed for a brief moment and whose gestures are confused with yours: the way you look when you don't believe me, the way you touch my body before you love, like someone who fears that something is going to break, in you or in me.

It was for a woman who might have been you, in another latitude, with another calendar. A woman who looked like you, but wasn't you. Or for all the women who carry you on their skin without knowing it. I wrote it on a night when it was raining in Scopello. You know those rains that don't clean anything, they just push the tears of longing against the glass?

I've never known how to write letters with a fixed addressee, because it's difficult to occupy a space that is there and exists. I write to the absences and to the versions of me that no longer come back.

And sometimes—almost always—you come mixed in, but not alone. Sometimes, on those occasions, you're like perfume on a scarf that I don't know if it's yours or if I bought it in a Moroccan bazaar on a mission to Rabat.

Don't judge me badly. Your answer hurt me with the sweetness that only you know how to hurt. You said you wouldn't come back and I believe you. You were always better at leaving than I was at staying. But I'm not asking you to come back, even though I miss you sometimes, a lot.

But tell me: if it wasn't yours, why did you read it as if it was? And why did you answer it like someone writing on a mirror in a hotel room, thinking that someone will come in and see it? You know who the letter was for. I know you do. It was for your reflection, but not for you.

Perhaps because you knew that, deep down, all my writing is a rehearsal for the moment when I see you again, or for the moment when I see her again. Or imagining that one day I'll see them both.

You stayed where I left you, at the exact point between lucidity and desire. But you were always smarter than me. You knew that love was dangerous. I, naïve, thought that codifying love would make it safer. But I never really understood how to love, not you, not your reflection and not the real recipient of the letter

I was wrong. As usual.

But tell me: wasn't making mistakes with you always the right thing to do?

Leilac

Vila Nova de Gaia, Portugal.

4

The Letter That Is Enough
Brescia, 2025, Signed Mariangela

Leilac, *cazzo*...
I read your letter in the morning, with my coffee lukewarm and my heart leaking like boiled milk, forgotten in a kettle, which ended up overflowing. I read it, reread it and swore I wouldn't reply. But here I am, burning my eyelashes with words that I make an effort to choose well, but which I know shouldn't exist. They are words that burst inside me like poorly aimed rockets.

You say that maybe it wasn't for me. Maybe it was for someone else. Fuck off with your "maybes", Leilac. You never knew how to be whole, not even when you lay on top of me with that look of someone who loved but couldn't fucking hold on.

That letter, that shitty letter that you hid in your suitcase like an important man and a grown-up kid, had my name scrawled between the lines. It was there in the curve of the "labyrinth", in the sly way you ask "hold me" without ever having said it out loud. But it was too late, wasn't it? You've always been better at writing than being, at pretending than loving.

You write like someone who spits charm out of every pore, but you lack blood. You lack bone. You lack skin. You're everything, but then you're nothing. Think about it: have you ever been real with me? Or have you always just been rehearsing for the next scene, the next woman and the next secret?

Damn it, Leilac, you were lavender-scented poison and I drank you like someone who wants to die slowly. You were my hemlock, which Socrates drank to escape having to lie and deny his values.

Yes, I loved you. With a fucked-up love, the kind that burns even when the bed is cold. But you? You've never known what to do with real love. You're good with codes, with strategies, with speeches for judges and orphaned children, but you're a lost child when someone loves you without hiding it.

Do you know what hurts me the most? It's that even now, while I'm sending you this blast of cursed words, I keep imagining the sound of your voice reading this silently, with that smile at the corner of your mouth that you wear when you know you've won. And you always win, don't you, *stronzo*?

But not today. Today I'm writing. And not with pity. It's with anger, with pain and with that kind of tenderness you only give to people you'll never touch again.

Go, Leilac. Go write your little books. Go teach Micas how to save the world. Go get involved in your luxury conspiracies, your mistresses with subway station names. Go be the paper hero you've always wanted to be. Go hide everything you drag around with you, from giant companies to even bigger hearts, in some story you write just to provoke. Your books are compliments, but they are also, and perhaps even more so, provocations.

But leave me out of it. I'm flesh, not a character. I'm Mariangela. I don't belong to you anymore and I don't belong to your secrets or your silences, even though you keep gluing me to your books.

Che basti.
Mariangela
Brescia, Italy, 2025.

5

Letter on My Knees
Palermo, Not Dated, Signed Leilac

Mariangela,
You said "hemlock" and I shuddered. Not because of the word, you know that words are sometimes armor to me, but because of what it brought with it. That image of Socrates, painted by Jacques-Louis David in 1787, his arm firmly grasping the chalice while the others, wracked with pain, mourn his lucid choice. You are those others, but you are also the chalice. With some shame, for me, you are still the old philosopher convinced that dying with coherence is more dignified than a life made up of concessions. It's nobler to die whole than to live in pieces.

But you didn't die, Mariangela. I pretended I was. I hid you in paper. But I never really killed you. I left you the quill and carried on writing.

You drank it all when I expected you to just wet your lips.

I read your letter as if it were the final sentence. And maybe it is. I know it is, or almost. The naked truth, unleashed with the fury of those who have loved on their knees and been left standing. You said you're not a character. That you're flesh. I know... and that too. I've known it for much longer than I or you realize. I know that I turned you into a character precisely because I couldn't bear your reality. Because you're too much. Because you're more than my paper can contain and more than my verbs can conjugate.

You were the only one I never had to decipher, but I never understood, and so I ran away. Because loving without needing a translation is scarier to me than a devil's puzzle, a writer's labyrinth or a game of cards with only hearts.

You called me *stronzo*. You're right. I am a *stronzo*. A coward. A scoundrel with a Moleskine notebook and a Montblanc ballpoint pen. A man with *offshore* accounts that more than protect money, guarantee my escape. You loved me like someone who throws himself without a net, and I... I was already writing the fall before I even held your hand.

But there's something you might not know, or maybe you do know and have pretended to forget in order to protect me: I died too, Mariangela. Not like Socrates, not with heroism, but with a succession of small deaths. Each time you pushed me away from your skin. Each time you left my bed before the lie had settled in. Each time you said "enough" and I, instead of fighting, picked up the pen and wrote a new chapter.

Now you tell me I don't belong to you and I accept that. But at least let me belong to the mistake, the failure and the memory. I also want to belong and be part of the pages you never read, where I drew you as a Madonna in ruins, as a Venus in armor and as a woman who burns and freezes in a single gesture.

You said *"Che basti"*. I, who have used words as weapons, have none to save me today. I'll just tell you this: if you ever see a man sitting on a stone bench, in silence, in any museum where the canvas of David is displayed just like the Guernica in Madrid, with the force of its absence of color and the portrait of war, if you see him, that man, staring at the gesture of the chalice, not knowing whether to admire or lament, you'll know it's me. Don't talk to me. Don't touch me. But look at me, just for a second, and remember that I was yours. Even if it's bad. Even if it's late.

With the ink I have left,
Leilac. Palermo.

6

Unanswered Letter
Rome, No Date, Signed Camilla

Leilac,
I was hoping for an answer. Not just any answer, from you. I waited like someone who knows they shouldn't, but waits anyway. Like someone who remains seated after everyone has left the room.

But now I understand.

The letter I wrote you... should never have left my hands. It wasn't a mistake. It was weakness.

You don't have to answer and please don't write again with longing what you were never able to say with courage.

Camilla, Rome.

7

Letters from the Past
Madrid, April 1, 2025, Leilac

The day began the moment I stepped off the plane. Madrid was boiling, as if it had it in for me. The city welcomed me as if I owed it something. I hadn't even set foot on the ground and I already felt guilty.

I caught an Uber outside the airport. It was a white Tesla, which in theory should mean comfort. But it smelled of unwashed breath and deodorant on top of sweat. The heat came in through the air conditioning as if the car itself was on fire inside. And there I was, with no desire to talk or exist.

I arrived at Cava Baja with the name of the hotel in my head: "Posada del Dragón", a name that had sounded good the night before, when I had hurriedly marked it with my eyes half closed and my memory soaked with you. But there, facing a tavern with letters painted on the brown wall, as if it were a Spanish telenovela from the 80s, I realized that I had screwed up.

There was a door with a blackboard menu scrawled in chalk, the smell of old fried food and some horrible music dripping from the ceiling. I went in. At the far end, where the counter ended and the bar forgot about itself, there was an embarrassed, shrunken reception desk, almost apologizing for existing.

I *checked in* like someone signing a paper to get in on a mistake. I went to put my bags down and try to freshen up. But that shit wasn't a charming hotel, it wasn't four stars like it claimed to be and it wasn't even an honest inn. It looked like an old whorehouse, one of those houses lost in Spanish pirate movies—where at the front there's the tavern for the drunks and whores, and at the back, in an embarrassing U-shaped courtyard, there are balconies and rooms with doors that groan with fatigue. All that was missing were the whores leaning over the balconies, wearing red dresses to match the color of the doors and missing teeth, laughing at me and saying *"¡hola, guapo!"* as if they knew what I was coming for.

The room, which they insist on calling *"deluxe"*, was a prison cell with pretensions to contemporary art. A twisted wire lamp, an orange telephone worthy of a Soviet *bunker* and a bathroom without a door, open to the bed as if you were supposed to shit with witnesses. I tried to laugh, but even that didn't come out.

But that's what I am too, isn't it? A guy who lies in beds where he shouldn't be, with people who only live inside his head.

At five I had a meeting with the Israelis at the Europa Tower. I walked. An hour of walking helps me pretend I'm doing something useful with my body. Nearby, before setting off, I shoved a sandwich with a *tortilla* foced down my throat. Bread inside bread. A sort of Spanish joke about life: putting stuffing where there's only repetition.

The meeting was quick. Papers. Greetings. Decisions like choosing the sauce on a sandwich—not very important, but with an impact.

It went well. So what? What does that change? Nothing could take away that feeling of being dirty inside. Not physically—really dirty, like when you come home and feel that the world outside has lost something fair.

I did think of you. But not with longing. With that new feeling that has no name—a mixture of shame, tenderness and anger at what we never knew how to say.

The second meeting was scheduled for 18:00 in the Salamanca district, Calle Jorge Juan—where Madrid pretends to be civilized.

Another half hour on foot. And my soul was dragging around inside my body like a sack of bricks.

I'd made a reservation at the Amazónico. That one. The original. Before its successors in Monte Carlo or Dubai. This was the one that meant something to me, because it still smelled of memory, mine, not *marketing*. I chose the sushi bar. I wasn't in the mood for the sequins of the fake jungle, just a stool, a man, raw fish and maybe a glass. I wanted the minimum, to leave room for the rest. The conversations. Between the lines. The possibility of you walking through the door and sitting next to me, as if nothing had happened. As if you were still mine.

But you weren't there. You weren't in the city, you weren't in my life and you weren't even in the plans. Which is understandable, the city wasn't yours and neither was my life. Nor did your plans intersect with mine.

I was tired of carrying the silence alone, so I had replaced you. The day before I had run through my electronic list of names with emotional addresses in Madrid. Sierra. Of course. We met right there, in that restaurant. A dinner date, I thought. An uncompromising reunion, perhaps with a minimum dose of nostalgia.

We scheduled it for twenty. But at minus eighteen, the WhatsApp message came: "Board meeting scheduled in a hurry", she was going, but didn't know when she'd be leaving. She canceled. With that light tone of people who no longer owe us anything.

I, who refuse to lose even when I'm already buried, insisted on the plan. I needed that dinner. I needed that night, not another. I didn't care about the company, as long as I talked. About you, about me, about anything that would take my mind off that whorehouse room I'd gotten myself into.

Quick *scroll* through the list. I fired off several messages like someone shooting into the air waiting for someone to shout "here". The first to reply was Grazia. I didn't remember her. I had her contact saved with a code that only I know how to read—a sort of archive system of shame, of the past or of good times, but ephemeral. I asked her who she was, I didn't remember her or the name that marked her phone number. She replied: "5'10" with red hair". Of course. We'd had something, maybe under the sheets or in the

25

bathroom of some bar. It didn't matter. "Probably," she said. "Would you like some dinner?" I asked. "My husband might not like it." I replied, "I'm not jealous." She laughed with an *emoji*. Time has turned us into caricatures.

Then I tried Severina. She said she already had plans. I insisted. I told her it wasn't about the next one, it was about this one. That the next one was too far away for someone who was sinking into a shitty day. She replied: "Anyone who's waited eight years to send me a message can wait another two for dinner." There was silence.

Five more names later and the void was confirmed. In the past, when we were all younger and more shameful, all it took was a "let's go" and everything would happen. Now, there are agendas, children, husbands and a certain weariness in the responses. And there I was, a man trying to save the day with some dinner, with no other intention than a fucking meal and company to put up with me. One hour, I didn't need any more.

The meeting was pushed back to 7:45. I arrived at the law firm fifteen minutes before the doors closed. Angel, who had come all the way from Santiago just for me, arrived first. Then Javier. The conversation was quick and clean. Everything was settled. I was supposed to be satisfied. But that feeling of emotional dirt remained glued to my bones and spread to the very surface of my skin, like moisture that doesn't dry out but instead seeps in.

And as if the day still needed kicking, an *email* arrived from Rodrigo Madrigal. The verdict in a small case—condominium *vs* contractor. A judge dazzled by a lawyer who had been Secretary of State for Culture for a few days, maybe less than a week. Probably seven days. How can seven days in power legitimize an absurd decision? That judge had other cases of ours. Important ones. She had screwed up in others too. The Supreme Court corrected it, but the psychological damage was done.

I walked to the hotel. Or to the whorehouse with Soviet *bunker* pretensions. Inevitably, I passed the door of the Amazónico. The reservation was still up and the place was probably still empty. I stood there for a second. I almost went in. But I didn't have the courage to sit alone at the sushi bar, like a guy who's missed the train of life but is still trying to have a good dinner.

I ended up in a street tavern. A stainless steel counter, white light and a fat lady with a moustache selling dry pies behind a fogged-up window. I ate six. Six. A kind of penance. I washed them down with soda water, because it was the only thing that seemed clean.

I went back to my room. To the cell. To the bed. The lamp flickered as if it were dying a slow death. The orange phone looked at me like a warning. I still have one day left in Madrid. I used to love this city, but all I could think about was getting out of here before it returned me to what I no longer want to be.

Leilac.

Madrid, April 1, 2025

8

The Surrealism of the Sentence
Madrid, April 2, 2025, Leilac

Rodrigo,
I'm writing to you from a grimy but friendly café near the Reina Sofía Museum in Madrid. The city woke up more slowly than I did—which isn't easy. I ordered a short coffee that came lukewarm and a tostada with tomatoes that already smelled of lunch.

I've just *checked out of* that simulacrum of a hotel, one with the reception camouflaged at the end of the counter of a tavern with the smell of fried food from 1987 and retired whores. I took with me the smell and an anger that grows in my stomach like mold on a dark, disgusting, damp wall.

But I'm not writing to complain about the hotel, it's the sentence. The fucking sentence.

That masterpiece of legal delirium.

That sentence that seems to have been written with a black pen dipped in contempt.

Rodrigo, what the fuck was that?

Let's get to the facts, which fortunately the judge, for her part, didn't manage to fudge:

- There was a contract.

- The contract said three months.
- The parties signed the contract with their hands, eyes open and full awareness. With the exception of that tricky and misleading clause about the percentage being the permillage.
- The public urban planning authority, Gaiurb, validated the execution of the work three months after the contract was signed.
- The contractor, this concrete artist, represented by a lawyer and writer, confirmed in writing, by *email,* that the deadline was three months. He didn't say maybe. He didn't say "let's see if we can make it". He said: three months.—Which, it should be noted, only reinforces the absurdity of the sentence.

And yet, the judge—in a gesture of creativity that would make a surrealist like Dali blush—decided that the deadline was actually six months. Why was that?

Because, you saw it, and you were certainly as astonished as I was, the building next door, with another condominium, another contract, another world, signed an agreement four months later that provided for a six-month term.

And, in the enlightened mind of the magistrate, this was enough to assume that our condominium, without anything signed, without any communication to that effect and without even a nod, tacitly accepted this new deadline.

Tacitly.

That word that in the judge's mouth served as a magic monopoly card: "advance to GO, skipping Jail, and collect $200".

Rodrigo, this is not justice.

This is bad faith mixed with legal elevator music.

The contract exists. It's written down. It's signed. It's been confirmed. It's there.

And she, in an argumentative pirouette worthy of a doped-up Russian gymnast, jumps over him as if he were an inconvenient step on the way to her private thesis of imaginary jurisprudence that favors the dazzle of a position of secretary of state, which isn't even hers.

What would Micas say?

Micas would say that this is like when you've arranged to have ice cream after dinner and at the last minute you're told that dinner will take three days, but you were already hungry that night.

I'd say it's not worth changing the rules of the game when the game has already started.

I'd say that "tacitly" is a word that adults use when they want to lie and appear correct and fair.

And you'd be right.

The most tragic thing about all this is that none of our arguments have been challenged. No evidence has been dismissed. The facts have been proven: the time frame in which the work was finished, after the three months of the contract; the *email* confirmation; everything.

And yet she decided the opposite of what she saw.

There is no justice possible when reality is seen, accepted and then ignored.

What happened here was not a mistake. It was an act of deliberate disobedience to contractual reason, to what is right and fair.

But the resource saves us from complete madness.

Your steady hand, the cold reasoning with hot blood, they're all there. I read it last night with the "cell" lamp flickering and the sound of footsteps on the stairs of the whorehouse in the background. And I felt a certain consolation. Not for hope—which is already lame—but for knowing how to say "enough" with elegance.

Keep going.

Attack with everything.

Not for me, nor for the condominium owners, but for everyone who still believes that signing a contract is useful.

Here I am, as always, ironic-tired and with a knife in my pocket.

Leilac, April 2nd, Madrid.

9

The Guernica
Madrid Airport, April 2, 2025, Leilac

Francesca,
A few hours ago I left that grimy hell where I spent the last night, a hotel that wasn't a hotel, a bed that looked like punishment and a mirror that always gave me the same look: that of someone who no longer has surprise on their face. I *checked out* without saying good morning. Hotels don't deserve words when they treat us like leftovers.

Yesterday, after the last meeting and a sentence that tore my idea of logic and justice like wet paper crumbling in my hands, I fled to the Reina Sofía. I did what I always do when Madrid treats me badly: I went to apologize to Guernica. Not to Picasso, not to art. To the painting. The painting itself. That wounded bull in black paint and charcoal.

I was on my feet for over forty minutes. Standing still. Staring.

People walked past me, took photos and commented on trivia as if they were looking in the window of a clothing store on sale. But I stayed. Immobile. Like a survivor returning to the site of the bombing.

Do you know what fucks me up, Francesca?

It's not just a painting.

It's a live autopsy.

Guernica is the last page of a diary written with broken bones and open mouths screaming inside, all seen from different angles.

There is no center. There is no rest. There is no hierarchy.

Everything runs over. Everything bleeds. Everything is simultaneous.

It's like our world. It's like my head.

I looked at the horse, its body distorted with pain, its tongue like a knife. And I saw myself. Me. Trying to get through these days with some dignity, but sobbing inside.

I saw you on the bull. Upright. Static. Hard as a penal code.

With that look you wore when you were undercover, but you knew that someone had discovered you. Toscin had discovered you, I had discovered you.

I saw the woman holding and mourning her dead son and recognized Maria from the door of your building—yes, even that—with the always deep eyes of someone who has seen too much injustice to be surprised by another.

And then there were the hands. Lots of them.

All open.

All asking for help, or saying enough is enough, or just confirming that they are still connected to someone.

I was there too, Francesca.

I also opened my hands.

But not to ask for anything. Just to drop what I was still carrying, and it wasn't light.

Guernica is made of grey tones because color would be insulting.

The color would pretend that there was still hope.

And there, in that painting, what there is is a world after the end.

A world where everything has already happened: disaster; betrayal; silence; and the repetition of what we knew would go wrong.

And yet everything keeps happening.

That's not a painting.

It's a map of emotions for anyone who knows how to read it, and it shows everything that has been lost and continues to move.

You know.

You, who have spent months undercover in the putrid heart of the mafia, know what it's like to live among monsters without letting your blood become contaminated.

You know what it's like to pretend that the mission is enough for you, when all you wanted was an honest bed and love without conditions.

The truth is, Francesca—and here I am being far too honest for someone who has to catch a flight—that I keep looking for Mariangela in the wrong women. In the right meetings. In the most unlikely silences.

I still see Mariangela in that woman holding the candle in the corner of the Guernica.

Not because she's the light. But because she's the witness.

You've seen the worst of me.

And you didn't run away.

But you also saw the best, the human and fragile side of our first night in the safe house in Ferrara.

And me... I'm just another person trying to make sense of the chaos, clinging to words and a blackboard like others cling to knives.

I'm going back. Home, yes. But also to you, soon, to Palermo.

I'll be in Palermo on the 17th.

I arrive in the early afternoon. I go straight to Scopello, as I always do when I need to remember who I am, or who I was, before all this, before looking at Guernica, today, this first time, after many others before. Because every time I look at it, it's like seeing something new, something I've never seen before. It's always different, not the painting, but the feeling.

Do you know the perfume that greets me every time I arrive in Sicily? It's that warm smell of stone in the sun and the tired sea.

The smell of walls that hold my happiest memories, the smell of hand-washed sheets, the sound of doors slamming in the light breeze just to confirm that they still exist.

Since I sold the safe house in Palermo, the one in Scopello is the only one that still recognizes me by my old name.

The only one where the water tastes the way I like to drink it, where the books still bear her fingerprints, Mariangela's, but also yours.

After all, they both passed through. Only in such similar ways that the house still doesn't know which of the two remained.

With Mariangela, that house was the rehearsal for what never happened. It was home to almost tender gestures, arguments interrupted by kisses and dinners that started too late to be innocent.

That's where there was almost a future.

And now it's just shelter.

Refuge without plans.

With you it was company, a friendly voice and, more than that, a shoulder to listen to and lean on.

So if you're around, or feel like it, maybe we could have lunch. Or dinner.

Nothing solemn. Just bread, wine, memories and eyes to eyes.

There are no hidden promises in this.

Only one clear desire: to have your presence outside the labyrinth again.

I want to see you smile with your eyes.

Tell me if you can.

Or if you'd rather not.

I'll be there.

Even alone.

Leilac

Madrid, April 2, 2025

10

If the Sea is Wild
Cefalú, April 5, 2025, Francesca

Leilac,
Yes, I'll be in Palermo on the 17th.
If it's dinner, better. If it's lunch, that's fine too. We can choose the day before, depending on what you fancy.

Reading your letter made my eyes water, as always.

Not out of emotion.

For defense.

There's always something in your words that grates, that makes you cry

I'm alone. I think I've already told you.

Since the separation. Two months, little more.

He left with a suitcase and didn't come back. There was no drama or shouting. That was it. Cowardice. Fear of the mafia, as soon as they found out about my past.

Another body got up and closed the door.

I kept the books, the wine glasses and the L-shaped sofa. I hope I don't become an alcoholic.

Sometimes I sleep on his side. Sometimes on mine.

It depends on the night.

I don't have anyone.

And it's no longer easy to have.

Age does that. It takes away sparkle and leaves lucidity, and lucidity is bad company for dates.

Beauty, that beauty we used to have in our own eyes and in other people's eyes, has evaporated. Almost fifty years is no longer twenty.

Now it's all in your hands.

In calm gestures.

Knowing how to listen without interrupting.

But that doesn't interest almost anyone.

I'm still doing my job.

I was called back to Rome, but I put it off.

They want me back, perhaps now with honors and medals. That's good. I feel that someone wants me.

But I'm tired. Tired of always seeing the same lies in new voices.

I need to walk slowly.

Palermo is the place to be.

See you on the 17th.

Don't bring me flowers.

Bring books.

I have bread and wine.

If the sea is rough, all the better.

Francesca

Cefalú, April 5, 2025.

11

Died Yesterday
Vicenza, April 5, 2025, Mariangela

A cute lymphoblastic leukemia, as you already knew. As we all knew
I went to see him two weeks before. He was barely talking. His eyes were there, but his voice was no longer his. I asked him if he wanted me to call someone, he said no. I even thought of you, honestly, because of redemption and mercy.

He made that gesture with his hand, the usual one, pushing the world away, as if to say: "Let me go as I came."

I stayed for a while. There wasn't much else to do.

I'm not writing to dramatize. Nor out of guilt.

Just to let you know.

He was. Maybe you were happy to hear the news. If there were people who hated each other, it was you and him.

In spite of everything, even with everything he did and did, my soul was broken. I don't know how to explain it. It wasn't love, you know that. It wasn't grief like losing someone you want to get back with, like I feel with you, alive. It was an old loss, perhaps of what never happened and could never happen. We weren't made for each other, as I am for you and you for me.

I've never loved him like I loved you.

He knew that. He's always known. He knew in Paris, when you showed up, when you came back with your "Game of Hearts".

And he never forgave me. Nor I him, for having wasted time wanting to love him without ever being able to.

Even so, at the time, we stayed. A little out of habit, a little out of silence and, above all, to get away from you and get away from how I felt about you.

It was easier that way. For me, but not for him.

Today, the house is quiet in a different way.

It had been quiet before. But now it's empty. Since you left, the house has been empty because no one else has come here or here. But today it's also empty of Mateo.

I don't know if you understand the difference. I think I do.

I'm not going to the funeral.

His family. Those who have remembered to show up in recent months.

I don't need to say goodbye. I said goodbye to him a long time ago, when he was still alive. Maybe not in the best way, but I left.

I'm writing to you because you're the only person who would understand this without asking me to explain.

And because, even though you're far away, you're still the name that comes to mind when everything else falls apart.

That's it.

Mariangela

Vincenza, April 5, 2025

12

Mariangela's grief
Chiclana, April 06, 2025, Leilac

Mariangela,
I received your letter with the slowness of someone who already knew what was written before opening the envelope. As if the weight of the words went through the paper before the ink. I knew Mateo was dying. I knew it would be now. I knew it wouldn't be for another month. I knew it... and I wished it.

Yes, I did. I'm not going to pretend I was noble. I'm not. I've never been with you and I'm not going to start now. I wished Mateo dead, with the cruelty of a wounded man and the coldness of someone who has lost everything because of someone who never deserved what he got.

Look, it wasn't just jealousy. It wasn't just the fact that he stole you away from me once, twice, three times, always with that poor little mangy dog pose, as if he was the victim of the story he wrote himself. It was more. It was hatred. A hatred that burned me inside and bit my nails.

He lied. About you, about me... about us. He played on your fear, your tiredness and your memory. And he played the son of a bitch well. Because he won. He won time. He gained presence. He gained a body next to you. And me? I watched from afar. Knowing that you were sleeping with someone you didn't love, but who knew how to keep you close.

In Capri, that day at La Fontelina. The beach full of tanned bodies, including yours and Chiara's, and the tourists pretending that life is eternal and me with him in the middle of the rage, I can't get out of my head.

That fight. That hand-to-hand fight that almost amounted to consensual murder. If he hadn't slipped on that wet stone, I would have pushed him harder. I don't know if you understand me. But I know what I did. I know what I was about to do. I know what I wanted: to disfigure him, until he stopped being someone, until he stopped being your past and a fucking obstacle between you and me. Until it no longer existed. And now... it has.

But a death is a death. And that changes everything.

Because death, Mariangela, is the end and the beginning. Not of the other. Of us. The death of someone who inhabited us, even when they were hated, even when they were unfair, even when they were strangers, shifts everything. It's as if they changed the floor of the room where we grew up and forced us to walk without knowing where to stand.

The truth is that we never know how to react to the death of someone we loved badly. Or of someone who loved us badly.

Mateo was your safe mistake. The transitional man who never left the place. A kind of furniture that you don't throw away because it's been there too long. I don't judge you. I've been worse. I've been the man who stayed because the other person didn't have the courage. I've been the substitute. I've been the break. I've been the wrong shoulder. I've been what you were with him.

And now he's dead and you've written to me. Worse, I'm here, answering you, not for him, but for you. Because I know what it hurts to lose even without love. I know what it's like to feel your body cut up by someone you no longer love. I know what it's like to miss what you don't want back.

But let me tell you something I've learned from making Micas grow through words written like seeds that take root to sprout flowers and bear fruit, watching women pass by, Grandma Mariquinhas, seeing everything fall apart every day just to keep going: mourning isn't about the dead. It never was.

Mourning is about what we are left carrying after death. It's about the questions we can no longer ask. The explanations that never came. The hugs we refused. The arguments that ended badly. The secrets that no one will ever confirm. Mourning is absence in full. It's silence with memory.

And nobody teaches us that. We're told to go to the funeral, wear black, don't cry too much or too little. To be "strong". A *cazzo* strong, as I'm sure you'd say. And then what? Then we're left alone with the ghosts. We're alone with that moment when we walk into a room and the smell is still there. Or you open a book and find a note. Or, even worse, you hear the person's name spoken by someone who doesn't know they're dead.

And the body trembles. Even though the mind says: it's over.

Fuck, you're still alive, you've just written to me and I feel it all. The smell, yours, that's missing from my room. That note from the opera "Carmen", the most attractive woman of all, with Marina Viotti, in Zurich, at the Opernhaus Zürich, which I keep inside a book in which you are the main character.

Mateo isn't coming back. Not ever again. And that's real. Not like the words. Not like photographs. Not like memories. Real like a cold floor or a hot cup. Like an absence that doesn't ask permission. Like an absence that doesn't knock, it simply enters.

But you can come back. If you want to. All it takes is for the goodbye you gave me to have a gap where our love can shine through. You can just come back, for real, in person and not in letters or mere memories. Come back, as if you were simply returning from somewhere far away. You can come back, come back, without explanation, as if you were returning in search of the warmth of an embrace and the salty taste of a wet kiss.

Come back, without blame, without questions, just with what could have been and what you want it to be.

I'm not celebrating Mateo's death. But I don't pretend to be sad either. I feel something else. A warm emptiness. An uncomfortable relief. A silence that isn't peace, but isn't war either.

But I'll celebrate your return, even if I'm running away from it. I'm a well of contradictions, I change my thoughts and desires with each new line.

And maybe that's what I'm left with: messy hope; the fear of seeing you go again; and the ridiculous courage to believe that this time it will work out.

Or, if it doesn't work out, at least let me believe that it will, for as long as it lasts.

Mariangela, you're in the middle of it. It shows in every letter you write to me. Come back.

But before you go back, let yourself feel everything: the sadness; the guilt; the relief. Let yourself cry for him. Or not. But don't pretend it doesn't hurt just because it wasn't love. It hurts. Because it was presence. Because it was the past. Because, despite everything, it was people. And that's enough to hurt.

But let it hurt more if you don't come back to me, until the pain becomes so unbearable that it's best to die or go back, which is exactly how I feel.

If you need me, I'm here. Not like before, but to receive you, as someone who comes back.

Mateo is dead.

But not you.

And neither do I.

Leilac

Chiclana de la Frontera, April 6, 2025

13

Old age, Reply to Francesca
Chiclana, April 6, 2025, Leilac

Francesca,
You said you're alone and I believe you.

But it's not the usual loneliness—that of someone who doesn't have company for dinner or goes to bed without any warmth. Yours is different. It's the one that comes after you've been everything. The one that comes after you've carried lives, missions, secrets, loves, dangers and survived it all. The one that comes after having been desired like water in times of drought and feared like a harsh truth. Your loneliness comes afterwards.

And that, Francesca, fucks me up inside. Because I know what that costs a woman like you. A woman whom the world used to look at with eyes of love and fear, but who now has to deal with the emptiness of someone who no longer looks, or if she does, it's to turn away. Because the beauty you have now—real, raw and distilled—can no longer be seen with the eyes of twenty years old. It's seen with the eyes of someone who has read too much and doesn't want to admit that they've lost the desire to reread.

You say that beauty has evaporated. No. The eyes that could see it have evaporated. The beauty that remains after youth is not taut skin, or tight hips and taut breasts. Now it's the beauty of wrinkles that have their own name. It's the beauty of hands that know where not to touch and where touch is more important and better. It's the beauty of bodies that have learned to ask permission without being submissive.

But we live in an age that has a horror of authenticity, just look at Instagram and see the filters that hide imperfections and signs of decay. Old age, even when it only says hello before settling in, like ours, is treated like emotional leprosy. Like a stain you try to hide with creams and Instagram filters. You and I are entering—crawling—into that territory where words are hard and silences are heavy.

I'm 48 years old. I say this slowly, because it's harder than it should be. Because only yesterday I was 34 and climbing stairs three steps at a time. Because just yesterday I saw you arrive at dinner parties in that black dress and I knew that no one else was going to take a deep breath in that room without thinking of you. Now I walk up the stairs slowly and think twice before ordering wine for dinner and even drinking water. Because reflux wakes me up at four in the morning and the urge to pee won't let me sleep straight through. Because the idea of going out to a party seems like an outrage to my aching body the next day. Because I no longer have the patience to wait for a stranger to ask me what I'm doing with my life when all I want to do is ask him what he's already lost. Because there are nights when I'd rather be making soup than drinking *cocktails* with ridiculous names. Because looks no longer linger, I no longer have those thirty that enchanted any eye. Because there's music that seems like a mistake and people who seem like actors from a weak script. Because there are clubs where I entered at twenty and left with stories, and today, I pass the door and only wonder if anyone there knows where the essence of fun lies. I don't dance anymore, Francesca, I dance. With more pauses. With more inward laughter. With more desire to walk, walk and walk under the stars, preferably by the sea. It's in this gentle rhythm that I realize: time no longer blows on my neck. It lives there, with a key, with a made bed and, sometimes, with nostalgia.

And more than that, I now see time eating away at my body as slowly as a bug gnaws away at wood from the inside. My bones ache for no reason. Mornings are hard to get going. The mirror is no longer my accomplice, but a witness. Fuck , I'm going to smash it to pieces one day, even with seven years of bad luck.

And that's not the worst part. The worst thing is knowing that there's more to come. That this is just the beginning. That what you feel—that sense of controlled decay, that fear of being dependent, that terror of one day having to ask people to wipe your ass—is real. That fucking life, in the end, is slow training for the humiliation of the body. Fuck, I'd rather die with a bullet in my ass. That's why I keep challenging everyone and everything, always waiting for that shot.

But I know that it's different for those who have children, for those who have other responsibilities, for those for whom one shot solves their problem of decay, but increases that of others, who depend on those who die. The end is not the same for everyone. We're not all the same.

You're afraid. I understand. Because so am I. What we are now is a kind of intermediate phase: we still have the old sparkle in our eyes, the agility to run up seven flights of stairs, or walk for two hours straight in Madrid or Paris, but our gestures are wearing thin. The nights of love, which used to last until the sun rose high, are now over before the moon has set. We're still desirable in specific contexts, but it's no longer enough to be in a room for it to tilt. And that... that's a brutal loss. A hard loss.

Nobody prepares us for irrelevance. To be the extras in our own story. To go from protagonists to mere footnotes in the lives of others, which only the most careful lawyers read and only to fuck us over. And yet, here we are.

I know about your incontinence, Francesca. I've always known. And I never said anything because it wasn't important. Because your body has always seemed more yours than any symptom. But I know that it hurts you. That there's a kind of shame that sets in, not because of what happens, but because of what it forces us to feel. The idea that the body that has always been a desire can become a burden. That it can embarrass, get in the way, stink and fail. That's the hell of conscience: knowing that time will betray you even inside your skin.

Yet here we are. Chatting. Arranging dinners. Ordering bread, wine and books. As if there were still time. As if the world wasn't pushing us towards the edge of the abyss with white gloves, like the Japanese push crowds onto a train. Is it the Japanese or the Chinese who are doing it? It doesn't matter, because life pushes in the same way anywhere in the world when it comes to old age.

But, Francesca, there's time. There still is.

Not the time before. Not the time that was squandered. But the other. The rare one. The time you savor without guilt and with desire. Time that isn't given to everyone. The time you don't spend with just anyone. The time we have left and which is the most precious. Because it comes after the end of illusion and self-deception.

You shouldn't be alone. I say this with the certainty that only comes with the years. You need someone. But not company. Presence. That presence that can't be explained or disguised. You need someone who knows your body and isn't scared—which I find very difficult, because you still have a wonderful body that will make many twenty-year-old girls envious. You need someone who knows about your scars, the ones on your body and the ones on your soul, and doesn't want to cover them up. Someone who will listen to you without haste and touch you without pity.

And that someone, Francesca, can still be so many people, him, who has left, me, or anyone else from the past, or someone from your present, or someone new, from the future. That's not what matters in this letter. What matters is that you don't accept less. Don't accept the men who smile but avoid what you were or what you are now. Don't accept those who pretend to listen but don't want to know. Don't accept those who praise your courage but tremble at your sadness.

You are made of another material, another claw, another skin and another bone. You deserve someone who understands you with their fingers and respects you with their silence. Who wants you even if your body fails you one day. Who won't give up when beauty retreats inwards—and that hasn't happened yet, your beauty is still there, the word of a man who knows how to appreciate it.

But maybe that's not in a husband, a boyfriend or a one-night stand. Maybe it only exists in Sicily. In that woman who gives you lemons and knows about your divorce. That old man who still calls you *ragazza* and has no ulterior motives. The bread lady who tells you: "Your eyes are grayer today" without knowing that it's because you slept badly.

Perhaps the answer lies there. In the raw earth. In the slow days. In the rough sea.

I'll be there. Day 17. I'll bring wine, bread and a book with worn-out pages. Maybe we'll be silent or maybe we'll talk until it's night and then continue.

Because talking to you has always been a way of postponing death. And maybe, if we talk too much, time will forget tell us the time.

Leilac

Chiclana de la Frontera, April 6,

14

Cards on the table
Lago di Como, April 6, 2025, Mariangela

I read your letter twice. The first time with anger. The second time with a sadness that pushed me to the kitchen floor at dawn, with an empty glass in my hand and my eyes full of water.

You could have been more human. You could have breathed before writing. But it's you. It's always been you: the man who gave me the world and then swept me off my feet with one sentence.

Yes, Mateo wasn't a saint. He wasn't even fair. He was weak in many ways and cruel in many others. But he was a man, human, Leilac. A man who lived, who suffered and now died. Now he is no more. But you, even knowing this, talk about his death as if it were a joke with bad *timing* and a stone finally kicked out of the way.

Talking about hatred is one thing. Talking about it with the cruel indifference of someone who seems relieved that they no longer have to fight for me... that's another.

He was a character in your books, yes. Don't deny it. You even put him in your labyrinths. In the middle of tunnels, dark corridors and dead-end decisions. He got into your puzzles and chessboards, in the middle of pawn gambits and other stories. You turned him into an enemy because you needed a villain. I think it was more like that, he was convenient for your stories, for your books. Because you knew you were the protagonist and you needed someone else to justify your silences, your fears and your absences. He was your excuse for running away from me. But he was also your excuse for coming back. He was there for everything, even what was contradictory in you.

Yes, I did. I let him into my life as a buffer. A break. A poorly arranged hiding place where I protected myself from the bang that was you.

But that doesn't make him any less of a person.

Don't reduce it to your anger.

You say that mourning is not about the dead.

It's about us.

Then let me do mine.

Even if he didn't deserve all the tears, he left memories in the corners of the "house".

Smells. Noises.

That particular way of dropping your shoes at the door.

Shutting up when he knew I just wanted silence.

You didn't understand, or didn't want to understand, that your letter wasn't just a reply to mine. It was also a reckoning. An open-book settlement.

But Leilac, sometimes life isn't a courtroom or a spy plot. You're always so litigious, so combative, so aggressive, especially in your words, even more so when they're written down.

Sometimes it's just someone who died.

And another who stayed.

And another who reads.

And someone who writes.

Yes, I'm angry with you.

Angry because you've managed, once again, to put everything at the center of your world. Your pain, your hatred and your right to hate.

And me? I stayed in the corner.

I kept the ashes.

I'm left with the memories you don't want to have.

But then, there at the end, as you always do, you left me the gap.

The one that holds me.

The one where you become you again. The real you. The one who sees me before I know I'm being seen.

You told me to come back.

You said you'd celebrate my return.

So, how do I answer you?

I'm telling you that I still love you.

Not in the same way. Not with that inconsequential fire of before. Now it's different.

Quieter. More full of wrinkles.

With fear. With memory. With tiredness.

But still love. A lot of love. A punished love that somehow wants to punish you.

I miss what we were.

What we were even when we pretended everything was fine.

I miss your eyes screaming when your mouth was silent, because you were always incapable of raising your voice, because you knew that your silences were much louder.

I miss seeing you wake up looking like you're already on the run.

I miss the way you knew where it hurt without me having to say it.

I almost hate you for still doing this to me.

But yes.

I want to go back.

I want to sit with you one evening in Scopello, without rushing, in the house you've rebuilt for us. Where the painting from the Paris gallery is, the "Trump of a Face".

I want to see the sea without having to speak.

I want to hear you say stupid, difficult and right things. Like you can, sometimes all in the same sentence.

I want to grow old in front of you and without disguise.

Maybe just for a few days.

Or maybe all the way.

But I want to.

Take wine.

Take bread.

Take that book you wrote to me in.

And don't bring flowers.
I don't want any funerals.
I want rebirths.
I want what's possible.
I want you.
The cards are on the table, play the way you want. There's no *bluffing*.
Mariangela.
Lago di Como, April 6, 2025.

15

Let's play
Chiclana de la Frontera, April 6, 2025, Leilac

Mariangela,
It seems that recently, no one wants flowers, everyone wants wine, bread and a book. That's a strange coincidence. Maybe we've finally realized, you, me, and others like us, that flowers are for funerals and farewells, and that they're as ephemeral as the joys of empty party nights or the glories that crumble like sugar at the bottom of a cup of coffee. Maybe that's because flowers wilt quickly and say nothing when they fall. Unlike wine, which warms you from the inside, bread, which is broken and shared, and a book, which lives on in your head for days after you close it.

Life is, after all, a set of tables with crumbs and wine stains that tell stories more real than any bouquet of roses that promised eternity and dried up in two days.

Your letter came to me on a day when I felt even older than yesterday and less old than tomorrow, I had just written to Francesca, who is having an existential and age-related crisis, she feels old, even though she's 48 or thereabouts. I felt that kind of weight on my back that comes from the body but is heavier in the head, a fatigue that can't be cured with sleep or relieved with coffee.

You say you still love me and I know you do, Mariangela. I know this the same way you know things that don't need proof, like the presumptions *jure et jure*, of law for law's sake, which can't be rebutted, don't admit proof to the contrary, because they're written on internal scars, under the skin and in the memory. It's one of those things, like the age of majority: you only have to turn eighteen and the law presumes, without any room for doubt, that you are capable, responsible and autonomous. Your love for me is like that too—an acquired, irreversible state that needs no further demonstration or testimony. It doesn't matter if you keep quiet, change country or name. Like coming of age, your love no longer depends on your behavior or your will. It's assumed. Absolutely. And no one can prove otherwise, not even you.

I'm 48 years old. It's not an age that one announces with pride, nor laments out loud. It's an age that you whisper about slowly, within a reality that weighs you down, that accumulates losses, disappointments and one or two tired victories. I'm successful, Mariangela. I have money, I have some academic status, I'm sought after for my unconcealed professional appetites and paid well for it, I have some social recognition, at least among my peers—but none of that matters to me. What weighs me down, however, is what I don't have: the immense emptiness that remains when the noise of the parties dies down, when the luxurious rooms are empty, when the contracts are closed and the applause fades into silence at some conference. This emptiness is what remains after the apparent glitter, when the pleasures we thought were essential turn out to be a fragile and unsatisfactory façade.

You talk about Mateo as if I had failed to feel the pain of his loss. Maybe you're right. But death, for me, is no longer a catalyst for easy emotions. Death, Mariangela, has become the most real and brutal metaphor for the finiteness of time, the constant reminder that everything we pursue so eagerly—money, power, *status*, all that shit—is nothing more than a desperate effort to deny our own mortality. Every funeral I attend, every friend or enemy who dies, is a ticking clock in the back of my mind, saying: time is now, live now, feel now. And I don't feel death as a connection, I feel it as a warning, a fucking aggressive reminder of the importance of the present.

The bohemian life, the endless nights out, the failed marriages—you know I had one, which I wish had never failed, not because of the marriage, but because of the person, the purest being I've ever met—were nothing more than desperate attempts to fill a fundamental emptiness, an existential boredom that pushed me into pointless battles, tribunals where you fight with sharp words and corporate espionage which, deep down, is nothing more than a sophisticated way of distracting your conscience from the lack of deeper meaning. Society applauds these battles. It considers them glorious and worthy. But society lies, Mariangela. It blatantly lies, selling us false glories, empty prizes and hollow trophies that gather dust and no lasting happiness.

You say I turned cold at his death. Maybe it's because I was forced to learn that reason and philosophy aren't enough to understand the depths of existence. I lived for many years believing that pure intellect would give me answers and that rationalism could solve the absurdity of life. I was profoundly wrong, because pure rationalism leads to sterility, an emotional desert, a silent nihilism that slowly erodes any will to live. It was then that I realized that the only thing capable of filling this void, of overcoming this brutal absence of rational meaning, is something profoundly irrational: love. Not an idealized love, but that visceral, chaotic, imperfect love that hurts as much as it saves and that tears us apart from the inside and rebuilds us with glue that fails and loose threads.

The happiness that wealth and status have brought me has always been temporary and precarious, like a house of cards erected on an unstable, shabby table—as it is with everyone, even if they deny it. The constant anxiety to keep up appearances, to follow social expectations, has become unbearable. In big cities, in high social relations, hypocrisy and artificiality are the rule, never the exception—you know this as well as I do, we live inside this world, perhaps even more you than me; definitely more you than me. Glamorous parties, elegant gatherings and superficial conversations in rooms scented with cynicism are only the backdrops for smiling masks and egos desperate for validation. I'm tired of it, Mariangela. I'm tired of the farce, the spectacle of human vanity and the frantic struggle for illusory power. Everything goes with time, age and death. This comes from books, from Tolstoy's novella "The Death of Ivan Ilyich".

And it's exactly in those moments, at the most extreme limits of human experience—when we are directly confronted with our mortality, with imminent danger, with devastating losses—that something purer, truer, reveals itself. It's in those moments that you realize that love not only exists, it's the only thing that really matters, the only thing that saves you from the absolute loneliness of the abyss. It's not death that connects me, but love. Love that screams louder, stronger and truer than anything else in the world.

Scopello, Palermo, the whole of Sicily, for me, have always been places where this truth becomes clearer, simpler and more authentic. For Don Pablo, my good friend, that place is Viana do Alentejo. For my sister, scraps from my bones, it's in Vila Nova de Gaia, by the sea. For Paula, my proxy friend, it's in Tuscany. For Mia, who stopped talking to me because of you, it's in a small village near Saint Tropez or in Tunisia. For Rodrigo, it's in Cape Verde, far from the courts and close to the sea and the essence of life. For Camila, it's with Jasmin, in Le Levandou. Everyone has their own place, where they don't need masks. For me, it's among fishermen and bread sellers, between *pistacchio* and *arancina*, between *gelato* and *pizza*, among simple people who know how to live with little, where there is an authenticity that no big city can offer. It is in these places, in these people who live with the disarming clarity of simplicity, that I find real meaning. In the way they look me in the eye with no ulterior motives, in the way they tell me the truths that hurt to hear, but that we need to listen to.

You say you want to come back. Then come back, Mariangela. Come back and let's live without masks. Let's live with bread, wine and books. Let's let time age us together, with honest wrinkles and true memories. Let's embrace the complexity of life without illusions, but with the courage of those who know that happiness is not a constant state of ecstasy, but a deep, visceral acceptance of the pains and joys that make us human.

The truth is that we grew up the other way around—first we shattered the illusion and then we realized that it was possible to love after that.

Perhaps this is the purest form of love: the one that remains when all the stories and excuses fail. The one that remains when desire is emptied from the theater and all that's left is the bare stage, with its worn boards and visible nails. Then you see who is left and why. The love that stays when there are no more promises, no more plans for the future and no more plans with a set date. The love that lives in the present, in the gesture, in the gaze that has seen it all and still chooses to stay. No guarantees, no armor and no theater.

I speak to you not as a man looking for redemption, but as someone who has been through the fire and now warms himself in the embers that remain. There is a raw beauty in what has resisted burning. And we, Mariangela, resisted. Even apart, even silent and even wrong. And that says more than any letter can tell.

Today, sitting in a café in Chiclana, dying to go to Scopello, I don't feel nostalgia. I feel presence. The stones know more about me than the mirrors, they give me back the image that others don't see.

I want to go back to our house in Sicily, the one I stubbornly hide from everyone and everything, but not from you, because it's ours, it has our picture, the "Trump of a Face". There I realized that faith doesn't have to be in God or dogma. It can be in a lady who gives me figs on an old Piaggio APE with an open box and worn-out paint parked in the square and asks me if I slept well. It could be in a kid running after a dog. It could be in you, when you write to me without frills or trick questions.

So, Mariangela, if you come back, let it be to live without theatrical arguments or excuses with footers and *disclaimers*. Come to be and not to act. Bring your silences, your fears and even your silly jealousies—but also bring your hands free, your heart available to me and your eyes clear. Come to share the table and not the altar. Come to share the bread and not the guilt.

And if you don't come back—and you might not—at least keep this letter, which is neither a request nor an invitation, but a testimony. Not of what we were, but of what we still are when we take everything else away. Two humans who recognize each other. And that's enough.

Appointment for Scopello. April 17th, after 3pm.

You've got the key to the door—it's new, it still scratches a little as it goes into the lock, the edges are rough, like the words we didn't say in time.

Come in. Put your coat down on the kitchen chair. Open the windows, let the sea in and let the wind rustle the papers on the table, as it always did.

The fridge is probably empty, but there's always wine on the bottom shelf of the cupboard. The green towel is still in the usual drawer.

Wait for me. If I arrive first, I'll wait for you.

No rehearsed words. No questions. Just presence.

That's all. Which, after all, is everything.

Leilac

Chiclana de la Frontera, April 6, 2025.

Afterword

They say that a book ends when you turn the last page. That's a lie.

A book like this doesn't end. You lean against the edge of what's missing and wait

Scopello is still missing. Scopello hasn't happened yet. Not yet.

And so this book—like me—remains unfinished.

It remains suspended between what has been said and what has been written so that it doesn't have to be said.

It continues between letters that have not been read, between voices that have not arrived and between perfumes that have not been repeated.

The sea is missing.

Scopello's sea, the one that doesn't need to be angry to be indomitable.

The sea that doesn't answer, but listens.

Who doesn't judge, but drags.

The sea that witnessed the cleanest silences and the dirtiest kisses.

The sea, which saw me fall to my knees—not out of devotion, but out of weakness.

And she's missing.

The woman who will make the period or the new paragraph.

Is it Francesca, with the eyes of someone who has seen too much and still wants to see more?

Is it Mariangela, with her thorny silences and words that burn like pure, coarse salt in a poorly washed wound?

Or is it the APE woman who offers me figs and asks me if I've slept well, as if she doesn't know I've slept like shit just by looking at my face?

Could it be one of them?

Is it none?

Is it the weather?

Is it the emptiness?

I don't know.

But I do know this: I've written everything I can so far.

I wrote with my body, with my eyes burned by the early hours of the morning and with my fingers tearing the paper as if there were skin underneath.

And now... we just have to wait.

Scopello is still waiting for me. She'll always wait. She's the only one who doesn't run away.

With its smell of hot stone and rotten lemon, with its stray dogs and the old man at the bar who calls me "*dottore*" without knowing why.

There, perhaps what has been left unresolved here will happen.

Or maybe not.

Maybe what happens in Scopello shouldn't be written down.

Just lived.

Or just supported.

This book, if it ever ends, will be there. Or maybe after.

On that balcony facing the blue that promises nothing.

If she comes, I'll write another chapter. The one in this book, but with a new life.

If she doesn't come, I'll write the same chapter again, but in a new book, with the same shitty life as always: without her.

In the same words.

With more anger.

Or more tenderly.

But I will write.

Because I still haven't learned another way to breathe.

Scopello, you have yet to live and write.

If you like this book, you might also like the "Game of Hearts", "The Writer's Labyrinth", the "Pawn Gambit" and the "Devil's Puzzle". Although this is a sequel, all five books can be read independently. The previous four books set the stage for the letters in this book, introducing the characters and the captivating universe they inhabit.

Each book offers a unique and immersive experience, so whether you start with the first, second, third, fourth or this one, you're about to embark on an exciting journey, full of depth, mystery and lots of love.

Explore these interconnected stories and discover how each piece, whether it's a chess piece, a puzzle piece, a maze piece or a card game piece, fits each word on these letters, no matter where you choose to start.

Contents

This book has been produced in line with the EU GPSR guidelines about the safety of products.

The General Product Safety Regulation is the European Union's updated framework for ensuring that all consumer products, including books, are safe for consumers.

This book has been printed by CPI books GmbH. The printer has issued safety certificates for the materials - like ink, paper and glue - being used.

The product identifier is: 9789403798219

The author is responsible for the content of the book, is the publisher of the works and bears full responsibility for it.

The book has been produced via Bookmundo. Bookmundo enables any author to share their stories with the rest of the world via printed books and ebooks and a broad distribution network.

Bookmundo will act as an intermediary in regard to questions about safety and will address them to the printer / author. Should there be any question in regard to the safety of the product, please contact us.

Bookmundo
Delftsestraat 33
3013AE Rotterdam
The Netherlands
info@bookmundo.com

Zeitfracht Medien GmbH
Ferdinand-Jühlke-Straße 7
99095 Erfurt, Deutschland
produktsicherheit@kolibri360.de